# BUNNY ROMERO'S
# WHITE HOUSE ADVENTURE
## THE WHOLE MEGILLAH!

Written by **MARGIE BLUMBERG** • Illustrated by **RENÉE ANDRIANI**

MB PUBLISHING

**For My Parents,**
who happily shared their love for rhymes, stories, languages,
geography, history, genealogy — and hamantashen!

**For White House Chef Walter Scheib (1954–2015),**
who graciously led a personal tour of the White House. Because of his
generosity, my wish to eat a tuna fish sandwich in the kitchen came true!

~Margie

To all those who come to America and make our country a better place.

~Renée

---

Parents and teachers: **Children might enjoy looking for images that symbolize the two holidays featured in this book.**

*Images of Purim* ~ Bunny's Queen Esther costume • Bunny's and Benjy's crowns • hamantashen (cookies) • Ms. Maven's scroll of rules and the scroll at the end of the story (to bring to mind the scroll read at Purim) • Ms. Maven's noisemakers (like the groggers that are shaken and twirled to drown out the name of Haman while reading the *Megillah*)

*Images of Thanksgiving* ~ the fall season: leaves and berries and pumpkins • Tater the turkey (though he is a pet, not dinner) • apple pie • cornucopia

Note: President Thomas Jefferson (Green Room), President Martin Van Buren (Blue Room), and President James Knox Polk and First Lady Sarah Childress Polk (Red Room) are featured in the story to explain how the rooms acquired their colorful names. For information about these and other historical figures presented in the book — and for fun facts about the White House itself — please visit http://www.mbpublishing.com.

---

Text copyright © 2018 by Margie Blumberg/MB Publishing, LLC
Illustrations copyright © 2018 by Renée Andriani
Book design copyright © 2018 by PageWave Graphics Inc.
All rights reserved.

First published in the United States by MB Publishing, LLC

www.mbpublishing.com

Summary: Rhyming text in English, Spanish, Yiddish, and Hebrew
is accompanied by charming illustrations to present an eventful
day for second-grader Bunny Romero, her class, the White House
staff — and one fun-loving turkey.

Library of Congress Control Number: 2018902651

Blumberg, Margie
Bunny Romero's White House Adventure: The Whole Megillah!/
by Margie Blumberg; illustrations by Renée Andriani

ISBNs:
Softcover: 978-0-9994463-2-4
Kindle: 978-0-9994463-0-0

**More MB Books**
*Rome Romp!* • *Paris Hop!* • *A Gefilte Fishy Tale* • *Sunny Bunnies* •
*Breezy Bunnies* • *No Naptime for Janie! A Hanukkah Tale* • *Avram's Gift*

# The Whole Megillah about the Word *Megillah*

President Abraham Lincoln once said that immigrants are the "wealth and strength" of our nation. And he was right. They bring with them their dreams, their talents, and their cultures, including language. Take, for instance, the word *megillah*. It is a Hebrew word that was at first simply used to mean "scroll," a kind of book that contains a story. The most famous *megillah* is the one that relates the tale of Queen Esther, the heroine celebrated during the Jewish festival of Purim. Happily for English, the "whole megillah" was adopted in 1957 with good humor to mean "the whole thing." As the granddaughter of immigrants who adopted America as their home, I hope that people will always be welcomed and protected here.

—*Margie Blumberg*

*adiós* (S) ~ goodbye (ah•**deeyohs**)

*ah, gracias* (S) ~ ah, thank you
(ah **grah**•seeyahs)

*amigos* (S) ~ friends (ah•**mee**•gohs)

*bella luna* (S) ~ beautiful moon
(**beh**•yah **loo**•nah)

*bissel* (Y) ~
little bit (**biss**'l)

*buenas noches* (S) ~
good night (**bweh**•nahs **noh**•chehs)

*castillo* (S) ~ castle (kah•**stee**•yoh)

*cierra tus ojos* (S) ~ close your eyes (see•**ehr**•ah
toose **oh**•khohs; kh = ch in Scottish *loch*)

*hamantashen* (Y) ~ literally, "Haman's pockets";
triangular cookies filled with jam, fruit, chocolate, or
a mixture of poppy seeds and honey that are enjoyed
throughout the year but prepared especially for
the festival of Purim (AE: **hah**•muhn•tah•shuhn;
singular, hamantash: **hah**•muhn•tahsh)

*keppy* (English diminutive of Yiddish diminutive
*kepeleh*, from *kop*: "head") ~ sweet little head
(**kehp**•ee; **kehp**•eh•leh)

**Note:** S = Spanish; Y = Yiddish; H = Hebrew; E = English; AE = American English

*la Casa Blanca* (S) ~ the White House (lah **kah**•sah **blahn**•kah)

*magnifico* (S) ~ magnificent (mag•**nee**•fee•koh)

*megillah* (H) ~ literally, "scroll"; it especially refers to the Book of Esther; also, a long explanation or story: the whole megillah (AE: muh•**gil**•uh; H: muh•gee•**lah**)

*mi nombre* (S) ~ my name (mee **nohm**•breh)

*nosh, noshing* (Y) ~ a snack, to snack (*nosh* rhymes with *gosh*)

*oy vey* (Y) ~ an exclamation of dismay, grief, or exasperation (*oy* rhymes with *toy*; *vey* rhymes with *day*)

*perfecto* (S) ~ perfect (pehr•**fehk**•toh)

*por favor* (S) ~ please (pohr fah•**bohr**; like the *b* in *bore*, but softer)

*Purim* (H) ~ the Jewish Festival of Lots, celebrated on the 14th day of the month of Adar to commemorate the saving of the Jews in Persia from destruction by Haman; the word *Purim* means "lots," which refers to the lottery that Haman used to select the date for carrying out his wicked plan; the story is recorded in the Book of Esther (*Megillat Esther*, in Hebrew), named for the queen who rescued her people (AE and Y: **poor**•im; H: poo•**reem**)

*Thanksgiving* (E) ~ the fourth Thursday in November in the United States celebrated as a legal holiday for people to express thanks for what they have (thangks•**giv**•ing)

*todah* (H) ~ thank you (toh•**dah**)

**Bunny Romero — a new immigrant from Mexico —
had one special wish. This is her story . . . the whole megillah!**

It all began one snowy Purim in early March. Bunny was enjoying the gifts her nana had sent her all the way from Mexico City: sweet hamantashen and a beautiful book.

"*Magnifico,*" Bunny sighed when she saw a photo of the White House. It reminded her of the elegant cakes that she and her nana used to make. That's when Bunny decided:

"Someday, I'm going to eat Nana's hamantashen in the kitchen of this magnificent place!" And in a whisper, she added, "Maybe then I'll *really* feel at home in my new country."

The only tricky part was that Bunny didn't know how such a wish could come true.

Six months later, when her second-grade teacher announced that the class would be touring the White House right before Thanksgiving, all the children erupted in applause. Bunny clapped the loudest.

**And when that fateful morning finally arrived, she exclaimed . . .**

"The White House — I'm ready —
My dream's coming true!"

"Three rooms — can you count them?
One oval, two squares.
They're bursting with paintings
And tables and chairs."

"But Benjy, the kitchen's
The best of the bunch
'Cause that's where I'll nosh on
My hamantash lunch!"

"Ah, *gracias*, thank you.
A pencil! I'm set ...
Except for some water —
Don't let me forget."

Honk-honk!

"I spy a gorilla
That's leaving the zoo."

"And temples of marble
For presidents, too."

"*Castillo* — a castle —
Huge columns, fresh paint.
I'm covered in goosebumps . . .
I hope I don't faint!"

"Be courteous, children.
No gabbing, no giggling.
Our building holds treasures —
Be gentle ... no wiggling."

"The Green Room, the Blue Room,
The Red Room await.
The hour is flying —
We mustn't be late!"

"By spreading some fabric
Beneath his wood table,
Tom Jefferson handed
This room its green label."

"He feasted on forkfuls
Of pasta with cheese
And spoonfuls of pound cake
With ice cream ..."

"This suite *was* called 'Oval,'
But that wouldn't do
When Martin Van Buren
Declared, 'I like blue!'"

"The Polks adored red —
Be it ruby or cherry.
And no other color
Could make them as merry!"

THE STATE DINING ROOM

"Imagine a banquet
Where, toasting sincerely,
Our hero Abe Lincoln
Said, 'Welcome,' quite clearly."

"Enjoy your Thanksgiving —
Don't stuff yourself silly.
Buh-bye, travel safely,
Zip up — it's still chilly."

*"Adiós? We're all done?
We can't depart now.
The kitchen's so close...
I'll get there somehow!"*

"Your tour was fantastic!
You're simply divine."

"Please, *por favor*, Bunny,
Come *back* right away!"

"Ring out when you spot her.
And hurry — *oy vey!*"

From every direction
Their voices were shrieking,
"Hey, Bunny, where are you?"

"Stop hide-and-go-seeking!"

"The yard is gigantic!"

"Gee whiz, what a trip."

"This man isn't helping..."

"Be careful, don't . . . slip!"

And meanwhile, Bunny,
As fast as she could
Stepped over the threshold,
Moved boldly . . . then stood.

It suddenly struck her:
"I've *not* been invited!"
She ate in the shadows —
Still very excited.

"My dream has come true —
Now I just need a drink.
I can't find my cup,
But I'm sure there's a sink ..."

Rounding the corner
She muttered aloud,
"I'm thirsty, so thirsty."
Her words drew a crowd.

"Hello, are you lost?
What's your name? Have a seat."

"*Mi nombre?* It's Bunny.
I brought a fun treat."

"Your cookie is perfect —
The filling's delish!
Do tell us the secret
To this yummy dish."

"My nana once told me —
And she's very smart —
To be a great baker,
Add love from your heart."

The chef, nodding warmly,
Served Bunny a slice.

"Ooh, apple ... *perfecto* ...
With raisins — how nice."

"Let's join your *amigos*.
It's quarter to two.
They're bound to be anxious . . ."

"They're searching for you!"

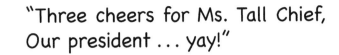

"Three cheers for Ms. Tall Chief,
Our president . . . yay!"

"And Danny, her son,
And his pet are united.
Wow, what an adventure —
We're truly delighted!"

"She *liked* Nana's cookies
And *laughed* at the noise.
She said we're a *grand* group
Of *fine* girls and boys."

"Kiss-kiss, rest your *keppy*.
I'll turn out the light.
*Cierra tus ojos* —
Sleep well, nighty-night."

But Bunny was twirling —
Her smile was wide.
"I can't close my eyes with
Such stories inside."

"Dear moon, *bella luna*,
I've oodles to share.
First let me get cozy
And snug in my chair."

*Buenas noches, Bunny . . .*
Sweet dreams!

And so, cherished reader, our story is done ...
Yes, that's what can happen with dreams, one by one.

Pursue what you're fond of, fill life to the top,
Do good, make a splash, share your joy — never stop!

# Dream Diary

What's your goal, your wish, your dream? Keep it in your heart. Jot it in your diary.
That's the way to start. Be it small or grandiose, silly, bold, or wise — dream a little dream
today . . . having one's the prize.

*Fill in as you grow, as soon as you know!*

# A *Bissel* of History

## Abraham Lincoln, Emma Lazarus, the Statue of Liberty — and Bunny Romero!

Mexican-born Bunny Romero and fourth-generation American Emma Lazarus have something in common: they are both descendants of Sephardim — Spanish and Portuguese Jews. Bunny's ancestors came from Spain. Emma's ancestors came from Portugal and were among America's first Jewish settlers. Her distinguished relatives included Moses Seixas (1744–1809) and Associate Justice of the U.S. Supreme Court Benjamin Cardozo (1870–1938).

When Emma was just 14 years old, President Abraham Lincoln proclaimed that immigrants are the "wealth and strength" of our nation. Perhaps she recalled these words 19 years later, when she worked as a volunteer with the Hebrew Immigrant Aid Society (HIAS) and dedicated herself to improving the lot of Jewish refugees from Russia. Emma raised money, set up English classes and a trade school, and provided essentials like food and clothing. One year later, these personal experiences fueled her inspirational poem, "The New Colossus," which she penned to raise money for the construction of the Statue of Liberty's pedestal.

To learn more, read *Liberty's Voice: The Story of Emma Lazarus* (Puffin Books, 2011). To learn about HIAS, visit www.hias.org.

In 1903, a bronze plaque engraved with Emma's poem was installed in the Statue of Liberty Museum, located inside the pedestal. The last five lines are best known, but the poem in its entirety is well worth taking to heart, as it so completely illuminates America's dedication to sanctuary.

# The New Colossus

**By Emma Lazarus (July 22, 1849 – November 19, 1887)**

Not like the brazen giant of Greek fame,

With conquering limbs astride from land to land;

Here at our sea-washed, sunset gates shall stand

A mighty woman with a torch, whose flame

Is the imprisoned lightning, and her name

Mother of Exiles. From her beacon-hand

Glows world-wide welcome; her mild eyes command

The air-bridged harbor that twin cities frame.

"Keep, ancient lands, your storied pomp!" cries she

With silent lips. "Give me your tired, your poor,

Your huddled masses yearning to breathe free,

The wretched refuse of your teeming shore.

Send these, the homeless, tempest-tost to me,

I lift my lamp beside the golden door!"

*Liberty Enlightening the World*

# It's Hamantashen Time!

As Purim approaches, you'll know what to do, 'cause this is the recipe — crafted for you!

**G**ather your crown and your scepter and listen: In the 4th century B.C.E., the Jewish people living in Persia (Iran) faced danger but were saved because of the courage of Queen Esther, who was helped by her cousin, Mordecai.

**L**ovingly bestow gift baskets of food or drink on family and friends and donate money to the needy.

**A**ssemble to hear the reading of the *Megillah*. Make noise with groggers to drown out the name of Haman, who threatened the Jews.

**D**iscover from the story of Purim how evil bigotry is and realize that it's our responsibility to act with kindness towards others.

**D**ress up in costumes while enjoying contests and games at carnivals.

**E**at a festive meal — featuring kreplach and turkey.

**N**osh on hamantashen for dessert. When eaten at any other time of the year, you may call them *noshen-tashen* (snack pockets)!

## INGREDIENTS
### Yields about 30 cookies

$2/3$ cup (10 tablespoons + 2 teaspoons) grass-fed unsalted butter, softened*

$1/2$ cup sugar

Ener-G egg replacer (or 1 egg):
$1\frac{1}{2}$ teaspoons replacer powder +
2 tablespoons warm water = 1 egg

3 tablespoons water

$1/2$ teaspoon organic vanilla

$2\frac{3}{8}$ cup + 4 teaspoons gluten-free Brown Rice Flour Superfine by Authentic Foods (or $2\frac{1}{2}$ cups all-purpose unbleached flour or another flour of your choice)

$3/4$ cup (36 level teaspoons) of filling — choose one or use a variety: fruit spreads, jams, or preserves (e.g., apricot, raspberry, fig) • mohn (honey-sweetened poppy seeds) • chocolate chips • nut butters

## INSTRUCTIONS

**IN A BOWL,**\*\* using a wooden spoon, cream the butter and sugar.

**ADD** the egg replacer (mix egg replacer and warm water thoroughly before adding to the butter-sugar mixture) and cream until smooth.

**MIX** in the water and the vanilla.

**SIFT** the flour and then mix it into the butter mixture until a ball of dough is formed.

**DIVIDE** the dough and form into two cylindrical logs, 3 inches in diameter each.

**WRAP** in plastic wrap and refrigerate for 2 hours.

**PLACE** an oven rack in the middle position and preheat the oven to 350°F.

**REMOVE** one log of dough from the fridge. Allow to soften for at least 30 minutes. Then remove the second log to soften.

**DIVIDE** the softened log into $\frac{1}{8}$-inch slices.

**ASSEMBLE** each cookie one at a time: Lay the first dough circle on a flat surface and place up to one level teaspoon of filling in the center. Do not overfill.

**CREATE THE COOKIE:** Keep in mind that a portion of the filling should remain visible in the center when finished. With your thumbs, lift up the bottom of the dough circle and, with your index fingers, lift up the two sides and gently draw in and pinch together the top edges to create two seams; then, draw in and pinch together the two remaining edges to create the third seam. **Note:** Do not pinch the three corners of the cookie dough. To perfect your technique, please watch the video on our website.

**PLACE** the cookies on a parchment-lined insulated aluminum baking pan with rolled edges.

**SPACE** the cookies one inch apart.

**PREPARE** the second batch while the first batch is baking.

**BAKE** for 20 minutes, or until lightly golden along the edges and golden brown on the bottom.

**COOL** the cookies in the pan for 5 minutes and then transfer to wire racks to finish cooling.

**THESE COOKIES** are best served fresh, but you may store them in an airtight container at room temperature for a few days or freeze for a couple of weeks.

\*Soften the butter at room temperature for about 30 minutes.

\*\*Or use a food processor to make the dough.

This recipe was adapted from Joan Nathan's recipe in *The Children's Jewish Holiday Kitchen* (Schocken, 2000). For a wonderful selection of books about Purim, please visit PJLibrary.org.

"Benjy, get ready
'Cause readin' while noshin'
Makes happy things happen —"

"*Todah, hamantashen!*"

Proof

Made in the USA
Columbia, SC
01 August 2018